This book belongs to:

Moat House Children's centre
Little Sparks Group
Deedmore Road
Coventry
tel:02476 622158

25

Stuart Trotter

Greedy Grumpy Hippo

rockpool
children's books

For: Vicki, Lily, Edward and Tilly

Rockpool Children's Books
15 North Street
Marton
Warwickshire
CV23 9RJ

First published in Great Britain by Rockpool Children's Books Ltd. 2006
Text and Illustrations copyright © Stuart Trotter 2006
Stuart Trotter has asserted the moral rights
to be identified as the author and illustrator of this book.

ISBN 0-9553022-0-X
ISBN 978-0-9553022-0-6

Printed in China

Hippo looked out
of his window and said,
"What a lovely day for a picnic."

Hippo filled his picnic basket with...
sandwiches, apples, bananas, strawberries,
yoghurt, carrots, cheese, orange juice and
boiled eggs. "Yum, yum!" he said.

He opened his door.
He looked left. He looked right.
Good. No one in sight.

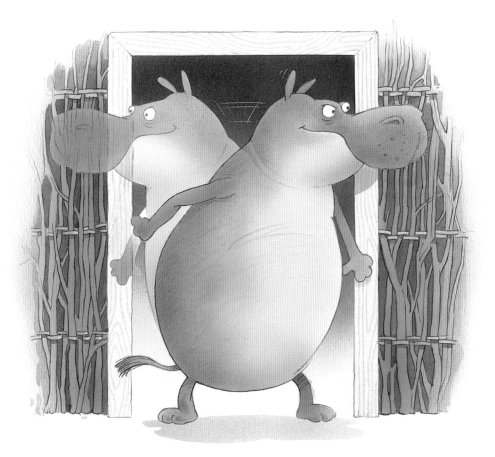

Greedy Grumpy Hippo wanted his
picnic all for himself.
He hadn't gone far when...

"What have you
got there?"
asked Monkey.

"What have you
got there?"
asked Lion.

"What have you
got there?"
asked Elephant.

"What have you
got there?"
asked Crocodile.

Alone at last!

Now what to eat first?

Hey, what's this?

Greedy Grumpy Hippo's basket was full of ...

Greedy Grumpy Hippo said,
"I'm sorry for being so greedy and grumpy."
And to show how sorry he was,
he shared his delicious picnic with
all the other animals.

He was indeed...

a very big-hearted Hippo.